A camping trip with an unexpected visitor

Encyclopedia lay beside Benny in their tent and checked his watch. At nine-thirty, Benny was still awake, still silent.

But at seven minutes before ten, faint snorts and heavy breathing arose.

"Did you hear something?" whispered Benny. "What was it?"

"What was it?" gasped Encyclopedia. "Yipes! I thought *it* was *you!*"

"L-listen," said Benny, as the noises came closer. "I think it's a bear!"

It wasn't a bear. It was a man stumbling about in the moonlight. His hands were bound behind him. He was trying to speak, but the gag in his mouth turned his words into wild snorts.

Encyclopedia quickly untied him.

"I'm Jack Evans," the man panted. "Bring help! At campsite five. Robbers! Kidnappers!"

For Paul and Elaine Furman

ABDOPUBLISHING.COM

Reinforced library bound edition published in 2015 by Spotlight, a division of ABDO
PO Box 398166, Minneapolis, Minnesota 55439. Spotlight produces high-quality
reinforced library bound editions for schools and libraries.
Published by agreement with Puffin Books.

Printed in the United States of America, North Mankato, Minnesota.
112014
012015

 **THIS BOOK CONTAINS
RECYCLED MATERIALS**

PUFFIN BOOKS
Published by the Penguin Group
Penguin Young Readers Group, 345 Hudson Street, New York, New York 10014, U.S.A.
Penguin Group (Canada), 90 Eglinton Avenue East, Suite 700,
Toronto, Ontario, Canada M4P 2Y3 (a division of Pearson Penguin Canada Inc.)
Penguin Books Ltd, 80 Strand, London WC2R 0RL, England
Penguin Ireland, 25 St Stephen's Green, Dublin 2, Ireland (a division of Penguin Books Ltd)
Penguin Group (Australia), 250 Camberwell Road, Camberwell, Victoria 3124, Australia
(a division of Pearson Australia Group Pty Ltd)
Penguin Books India Pvt Ltd, 11 Community Centre,
Panchsheel Park, New Delhi - 110 017, India
Penguin Group (NZ), 67 Apollo Drive, Rosedale, North Shore 0632, New Zealand
(a division of Pearson New Zealand Ltd)
Penguin Books (South Africa) (Pty) Ltd, 24 Sturdee Avenue,
Rosebank, Johannesburg 2196, South Africa
Registered Offices: Penguin Books Ltd, 80 Strand, London WC2R 0RL, England
First published in the United States of America by Dutton Children's Books,
a division of Penguin Young Readers Group, 1970
Published by Puffin Books, a division of Penguin Young Readers Group, 2008

LIBRARY OF CONGRESS CATALOGING-IN-PUBLICATION DATA

This book was previously cataloged with the following information:

Sobol, Donald J., 1924-2012.
 Encyclopedia Brown saves the day : ten all-new mysteries / Donald J. Sobol ; illustrated by
Leonard Shortall.
  p. cm. (Encyclopedia Brown books)
Summary: Ten mysteries for Encyclopedia Brown, his partner, Sally, and the reader to solve.
Solutions are given at the back of the book.
1. Mystery and detective stories--Juvenile fiction. I. Shortall, Leonard W., ill.
[Fic]
PZ7.S68524 Ers 1970

71-17149

978-1-61479-315-1 (reinforced library bound edition)

Spotlight

A Division of ABDO
abdopublishing.com

Encyclopedia Brown

Brown

Saves the Day

By DONALD J. SOBOL

illustrated by Leonard Shortall

PUFFIN BOOKS
An Imprint of Penguin Group (USA)

ABDO
Spotlight

Contents

The Case of the Electric Clock

Why did the police always catch anyone who broke the law in Idaville?

Only three persons knew the secret—Mr. and Mrs. Brown, and their only child, Encyclopedia.

And they weren't telling.

Mr. Brown was chief of police. Whenever he was asked about his success, he quickly spoke of many things. He spoke of Idaville's wonderful fresh air, its beaches, its three movie theaters and four banks, its churches and

5

synagogues, its Little League, and its two delicatessens.

But of catching crooks he spoke not a word.

The police department solved most of the crimes in Idaville, true enough. The hardest cases, however, Chief Brown brought home to his red brick house on Rover Avenue. Encyclopedia solved them while eating dinner.

Chief Brown would have liked to announce on national television, "My son is the greatest detective who ever climbed a tree!" But he didn't announce it. He didn't even whisper it.

What good would it do?

Who would believe that the real brain behind Idaville's war on crime was only ten years old?

So Chief Brown kept the secret even from the FBI. And people across the country went on thinking that Idaville had the smartest policemen in the world.

Encyclopedia never let a word slip about the

help he gave his father. He did not want to seem different from other fifth graders.

His nickname was another matter. He was stuck with *it*.

Only his parents and teachers called him by his right name, Leroy. Everyone else in Idaville called him Encyclopedia.

An encyclopedia is a book or set of books filled with all kinds of facts from A to Z. Encyclopedia had read more books than anybody in Idaville, and he never forgot a word. Really, he was more like a whole library than an encyclopedia. You might say he was the only library in America that closed at night to take a bath.

In the winter Encyclopedia did his detective work sitting in the dining room. When school let out, he moved to summer quarters in the garage. At his battered old desk by the gasoline can he was ready to help the children of the neighborhood.

Every morning he hung his sign outside the garage. It read:

BROWN DETECTIVE AGENCY
13 Rover Avenue
Leroy Brown, President
No case too small
25¢ per day
plus expenses

One morning Gil Tubbs came into the Brown Detective Agency.

Right off Encyclopedia knew something was wrong. Gil didn't fall over a thing.

Gil was Idaville's leading boy astronomer. He studied clouds, and he knew the names of two hundred and thirty stars. He could find the Big Dipper faster than his Sunday pants.

Usually Gil walked around staring up at the sky and tripping over porch steps and sleeping cats. But this morning he looked like any other boy—where he was going.

"What's up?" asked Encyclopedia.

"I wouldn't know. I can't raise my head," said Gil. "Last night I tripped over my desk clock and hurt my neck."

"Do you often walk across your desk at night?" asked Encyclopedia.

"I wasn't walking," said Gil. "I was running." He put twenty-five cents on the gasoline can beside Encyclopedia. "I want to hire you."

"To catch a runaway clock?" said Encyclopedia.

"To get back my telescope," said Gil.

He explained. He had awakened last night and had seen a boy in his room. The boy was climbing out the window with his telescope. Gil had leaped out of bed—and nearly knocked himself out.

"The thief had unplugged my electric desk clock," said Gil. "He'd tied the cord between my bed and the desk so I'd trip over it chasing him. Did I sail across the room! Wow! My head hit the wall so hard I thought I'd broken both my ankles."

"Makes my hair hurt just to hear it," said Encyclopedia. "When did this happen?"

"The clock was stopped at eleven minutes past ten," answered Gil. "I guess that's when the thief pulled out the plug. I don't have another clock so I can't be sure of the exact time."

"Did you get a look at the thief?" asked Encyclopedia.

"No, it was too dark. But I think it was Bugs Meany."

"Bugs!" exclaimed Encyclopedia. "I might have known!"

Bugs Meany was the leader of a gang of wild older boys. They called themselves the Tigers. They should have called themselves the weathermen. They never stole anything till the coast was clear.

"I'm not *sure* it was Bugs, mind you," said

Gil. "Mr. James, who lives next door, noticed Bugs outside my window a little after ten o'clock last night. He didn't pay any attention because Bugs often cuts through our yard to get to his house."

"Let's go and question Bugs," said Encyclopedia.

"Must we?" said Gil. "Bugs is awful tough."

"I've handled him before," replied Encyclopedia. "Get Bugs talking, and he'll cook himself in his own lies."

The Tigers' clubhouse was an unused tool shed behind Mr. Sweeny's Auto Body Shop. When Encyclopedia and Gil arrived, they saw a long line of children leading to the front doorway.

Several Tigers were keeping the line straight. Bugs himself stood by the front door.

"No need to push and shove," he called. "Everybody will get a chance to see the greatest little wonder of the twentieth century!"

The front door of the clubhouse had been

taken down. In its place was hung an old army blanket. In the center of the blanket was a small round glass, like a ship's porthole.

"One thin dime, kids," shouted Bugs. "That's all it costs. See the tiny moon man brought back by the crew of the Apollo spaceship!"

Encyclopedia and Gil slipped quietly into line.

One by one the children stepped to the glass in the blanket. They paid Bugs a dime and took a look.

"One dime," called Bugs. "See the moon man. He's so tiny that if he fell into a bowl of alphabet soup, he couldn't throw out an SOS!"

A girl called from the middle of the line.

"How is it that you have a man from the moon and nobody else has one?" she said. "The President didn't say anything about the astronauts finding life on the moon."

"The President didn't *dare* say anything," shot back Bugs. "Why? Because one moon man

The children stepped to the glass and took a look.

escaped! The President knew that a moon crea-
ture on the loose would scare the daylights out
of everybody in the country!"

Bugs paused to take a dime.

Then he said, "I found the escaped moon
man Tuesday night. He was hiding under an
old postage stamp on my porch. He's only an
inch and a half tall and his skin looks like green
cheese."

"Yeah, and he's got so many solid gold teeth
that he sleeps with his head in a safe," muttered
Gil.

"Sssh!" warned Encyclopedia.

It was too late. Bugs had seen them. He came
over and snarled at Encyclopedia. "Get lost and
stay there!"

"What's the matter, Bugs?" called a boy.
"Are you afraid of letting Encyclopedia see
your moon man?"

"I'm not afraid of nothing," shouted Bugs.
"Okay, Mr. Brains," he said to Encyclopedia.
"Step to the head of the line. You'll see the

greatest little wonder of the space age."

Encyclopedia and Gil each gave Bugs a dime. Then they looked. They saw a figure no bigger than a paper clip.

"What a fake!" whispered Gil. "The glass isn't a window. It's my telescope turned around so that you look through the large end. What you see appears tiny."

"Right," said Encyclopedia. "The moon man is one of Bugs Meany's Tigers covered with leaves and sea shells."

"You've had your turn," growled Bugs. He jerked a thumb over his shoulder. "Now make like a pair of headlights and hit the road."

"We will when you give back Gil's telescope," said Encyclopedia. "You stole it last night."

"But first you stretched the cord of my clock on the floor of my room so I'd trip over it chasing you," said Gil.

"I'll stretch your nose if you don't scram," threatened Bugs.

"A neighbor, Mr. James, saw you outside my window last night," said Gil.

"I was taking a shortcut home," said Bugs. "Say, when I passed your bedroom window your clock was still going. I heard it ticking. So the thief came after I had passed by."

Bugs suddenly moved close to Encyclopedia. His voice lowered.

"Listen," he said. "If you don't ruin my show, I'll cut you in for a share of the dimes. Sure, the moon man is fake. The kids are looking at Duke Kelly through the big end of a telescope, not through a window. But it's *my* telescope. You can't prove I'm not telling the truth about it. So why not join me?"

"I wouldn't join you if you were a circus parade," said Encyclopedia. "Besides, I can prove you're not telling the truth!"

HOW?

The Case of the Bird Watcher

Bugs Meany had one great aim in life.

It was to get even with Encyclopedia Brown.

With Encyclopedia on the job, Bugs and his Tigers couldn't get away with stealing so much as a leaky balloon.

Bugs hated being outsmarted. He thought a great deal about Encyclopedia's stomach. He longed to sock it till Encyclopedia hurt clear up to the roof of his mouth.

But Bugs never let fly a punch. Whenever he felt like it, he remembered Sally Kimball.

Sally was the prettiest girl in the fifth grade. And she had done what no other child under twelve had dreamed was possible. She had wiped the grass with Bugs Meany!

Bugs was bullying a cub scout when it happened. Sally told him to stop. Bugs sneered.

Sally raised her fists. Bugs laughed.

Wham! went Sally. *Plop!* went Bugs. When he got up, she dropped him again. Then she went to work in earnest. *Biff! Bam! Pow!*

After a minute Bugs reached an important decision. It was healthier to play the part of an ironing board than a prize fighter. He lay flat and stiff till Sally biked away.

Because of Sally, Bugs never roughed up Encyclopedia. Sally was the detective's junior partner.

However, Bugs didn't stop trying to get revenge. He only gave up the idea of using force.

"Watch out for him, Encyclopedia," Sally warned. "He's like a tube of toothpaste—the harder you press him, the more he tries to come out on top."

"I think he's in the middle of trying," said Encyclopedia.

"What do you mean?" asked Sally.

"Yesterday I received a letter signed 'Bill.' The writer told me to meet him behind Mr. Dunning's gas station at sunrise this morning," said Encyclopedia. "He enclosed twenty-five cents."

"Did you go?"

"Sure," said Encyclopedia. "But nobody showed up."

"I'll bet Bugs wrote the letter," said Sally. "It's some kind of plan to get you in trouble."

"We'll know in a minute," said Encyclopedia. "Here he comes."

A police car had stopped in front of the Brown garage. Officer Rand and Bugs climbed out.

"That's him!" shouted Bugs, pointing at Encyclopedia. "Mr. Goody-Goody himself! He let the air out of the tires of Mr. Dunning's truck this morning. I saw him, the dirty little sneak."

"Where were you at sunrise this morning?" Officer Rand asked Encyclopedia.

Bugs groaned and rubbed his ears.

"Why . . . I was at Mr. Dunning's gas station," replied Encyclopedia. "I saw his tow truck parked in back, but I didn't touch it."

"Man, oh man!" cried Bugs. "If lies were peanuts, this kid could choke a hippo with a flip of the lip."

"Cool off, Bugs," said Officer Rand. "We'll get to the truth." He turned to Encyclopedia. "What were you doing at the gas station so early in the morning?"

Encyclopedia explained about the letter asking him to be there. All the while, Bugs groaned and rubbed his ears as if he couldn't bear to hear such a terrible lie.

"That's a mighty strange story," said Officer Rand when Encyclopedia had finished.

"Golly," said Sally. "Encyclopedia wouldn't let the air out of anything—except maybe Bugs!"

"Somebody let the air out of the truck's tires and gave Mr. Dunning a lot of extra work this morning," said Officer Rand.

"What were *you* doing near the station at sunrise, Bugs?" demanded Sally.

"I was walking toward the ocean watching the birds along Dade River," said Bugs. "I'd reached the station when I noticed Encyclopedia letting the air out of the tires."

Encyclopedia thought quickly. Dade River ran due east to the ocean. Walking along the shore, Bugs could see Mr. Dunning's truck parked in back of the station as he claimed.

"How long have you been a bird watcher?" asked Encyclopedia.

"All my life," answered Bugs. "I love to walk along the river to the ocean and watch the birds."

Bugs closed his eyes. He folded his hands over his heart. Turning up his nose, he sniffed the air dreamily.

"The birds are so beautiful in the peaceful early morning air," he said with a deep sigh.

"Oh, bring down the curtain, Bugs," said. Sally. "You couldn't tell a hoot owl from a tree squeaking. I'll bet you can't name four birds that come to the river in the morning."

Bugs grinned as if he'd been expecting the question. "Morning dove, cardinal, mocking-bird, and egret."

"He's right," Encyclopedia said.

"He could have learned all those names from a book," said Sally. "He's the one who let the air out of the tires. I just know it! He's trying to frame you, Encyclopedia!"

"Did you hear that?" Bugs said to Officer Rand. "I told you they'd try to pin this on me. Nobody understands the real Bugs Meany. I'm just a simple nature boy under all this muscle."

Officer Rand shook his head. "I don't know which one of you to believe," he said.

"Bugs is lying," insisted Sally. "Encyclope-dia can prove it."

Then, realizing that she had spoken too quickly, she turned to the boy detective. "You can prove Bugs is lying about seeing you let the air out of the tires, can't you?"

"Certainly," said Encyclopedia. "Bugs wasn't bird-watching this morning."

HOW DID ENCYCLOPEDIA KNOW?

(Turn to page 88 for solution to The Case of the Bird Watcher.)

The Case of the Kidnapped Pigs

The day before the Idaville pet show, Lucy Fibbs and Carl Benton came into the Brown Detective Agency.

"Gwendoline has been kidnapped!" wailed Lucy.

"So has Alfred," said Carl.

Everybody in Idaville knew Gwendoline and Alfred. They were pigs. Gwendoline belonged to Lucy. Alfred belonged to Carl.

Few people had realized how smart pigs are till last year's pet show. Gwendoline had won the obedience test, which was the most important contest. She had defeated seventy-one dogs, cats, horses, parakeets, and hamsters. Alfred, the

25

only other pig in the contest, had taken second place.

Carl put twenty-five cents on the gasoline can beside Encyclopedia.

"We want to hire you," he said. "Find Gwendoline and Alfred."

"They were kidnapped to keep them from winning at the pet show tomorrow," said Lucy. "The Hurricanes took them!"

"The Hurricanes are four teenage boys who train German shepherds as watchdogs," explained Carl. "Were they sore last year when pigs beat their dogs!"

"Are you sure the Hurricanes did the kidnapping?" said Encyclopedia.

"I found this cap near Alfred's pen," said Carl.

He gave Encyclopedia the cap. The word Hurricanes was inked across the peak.

"One of the kidnappers must have dropped it last night," said Lucy.

"This morning I received a telephone call,"

"I'd know Alfred's grunts anywhere!"

said Carl. "The caller told me the pigs would be returned after the pet show. I wanted to be certain they were unharmed. So I asked to speak to Alfred."

"The kidnapper agreed?" said Encyclopedia.

"Yes, but first I had to call him back," said Carl. "His time was up. He didn't have another dime for more time on the telephone."

"A grown-up would have had plenty of money for the telephone," said Lucy. "The caller had to be a boy—a Hurricane!"

"I put in a dime and dialed the number he had given me," went on Carl. "Then I spoke to Alfred. I'd know his grunts anywhere!"

"Do you remember the telephone number?" said Encyclopedia.

"I wrote it down for you," said Carl. He handed Encyclopedia a slip of paper.

Encyclopedia read: *ZA 6-7575.*

"My dad traced the number," said Carl. "It is a public telephone booth out on Highway 37."

"We don't have much time," said Lucy. "We

can't look for motorists who may have passed a pig talking on the telephone this morning."

"You must question the Hurricanes today," said Carl. "You'll be able to pick the guilty one —or ones. I know it!"

"I'll question the Hurricanes, but I don't think I'll learn anything," warned Encyclopedia.

Encyclopedia left Sally in charge of the detective agency. He got on his bike and followed Carl and Lucy. They rode six miles out of town and into the farm lands.

"The Hurricanes train their dogs at the Smith place," said Lucy. "It's just down this road."

Soon Encyclopedia heard dogs barking. Rounding a corner, he saw the Hurricanes— Flip, Art, Merle, and Harry. Each had a German shepherd at his side.

The Hurricanes watched silently as Encyclopedia got off his bike.

"Did one of you lose a cap?" asked Encyclopedia.

The Hurricanes remained silent, watchful.

"Two pigs were stolen last night," said Encyclopedia. "A cap with the word Hurricane on it was found near the pen of one of the pigs."

"You've got some nerve coming here," said Flip. "We're not pignappers!"

"I'm not accusing you," replied Encyclopedia hastily. He eyed the four large dogs. "I'm only asking. Which one of you lost his cap?"

"Go drink some spot remover and disappear," snarled Art.

"Show them the cap, Encyclopedia," said Lucy. "It will fit one of them."

"Don't bother. We all wear the same size," snapped Harry. "Listen, I wouldn't know if I lost my cap. I haven't worn it for a week."

"Mine is in the front closet," said Flip. "I wore it two days ago when it rained. I saw it in the closet this morning."

"I loaned my cap to my brother," said Art. "He went to Glenn City Tuesday. Why don't you ask him?"

"I don't know where my cap is," said Merle. "But if you say I stole two pigs, I'll give you this!"

He shook his fist at Encyclopedia.

"If Merle hits you, you'll walk around like a pig on ice for two weeks," Harry promised. "Now beat it."

"I'm leaving," mumbled Encyclopedia. "Case closed."

"Encyclopedia!" cried Lucy in astonishment. "You can't quit!"

"You asked me to question the Hurricanes, and I did," said Encyclopedia.

"But you don't know who kidnapped Gwendoline and Alfred yet," protested Lucy.

"Wrong," said the boy detective. "The kidnapper gave himself away."

WHO WAS THE KIDNAPPER?

(Turn to page 89 for solution to The Case of the Kidnapped Pigs.)

The Case of the Bound Camper

Encyclopedia and his pals were going camping overnight in the State Park.

Encyclopedia looked forward to the outing —till Charlie Stewart brought bad news.

"Benny Breslin is joining us," said Charlie.

"Oh," said Encyclopedia.

"It gets worse," said Charlie. "Benny wants to share a tent with you."

"Oh, no!" said Encyclopedia.

Benny was a good friend—standing up. As soon as he lay down, he went to sleep and became a threat to the nation's forests. His snoring shook branches loose for half a mile around.

"I better bring my dad's crash helmet," said Encyclopedia.

"You better bring a baseball bat," said Charlie. "You might have to fight off a moose again."

Encyclopedia remembered the last camping trip. Benny's snoring had carried like a mating call. A bull moose had poked its head into the tent. Encyclopedia had chased it with a fishing pole.

"I don't have the heart to use a baseball bat," he said.

"I suppose you are right," said Charlie. "Any lovesick moose will suffer enough finding only Benny."

Encyclopedia left the baseball bat at home, and the two boys biked to Mill Creek. The rest of the gang was already there—Benny Breslin, Fangs Liveright, Pinky Plummer, Herb Stein, and Billy and Jody Turner.

Two hours later the boys reached the State

Park. After setting up camp, they hiked to the water to fish.

"Even if I land a torpedo, this trip can't be more of a bust than it is now," moaned Charlie. "Benny's snoring will keep us awake all night."

"Maybe not," said Encyclopedia. "If Benny sleeps all afternoon, he won't be sleepy tonight. And if he doesn't sleep tonight, he won't snore."

Encyclopedia chose a comfortable spot on the bank. It was better for catching forty winks than fish. He motioned Benny to sit beside him.

Benny settled himself till he was lying flat. "This is the life," he said. "I feel lucky . . ."

His voice trailed off. His eyes closed. Soon his nose sounded the opening notes of sleep.

One by one the other boys stole off to quieter places. They did not wake Benny until the day's catch had been cooked over the fire.

Later, Encyclopedia lay beside Benny in their tent and checked his watch. At nine-thirty, Benny was still awake, still silent.

But at seven minutes before ten, faint snorts and heavy breathing arose.

"Did you hear something?" whispered Benny. "What was it?"

"*What was it?*" gasped Encyclopedia. "Yipes! I thought *it* was *you!*"

"L-listen," said Benny, as the noises came closer. "I think it's a bear!"

The hair on Encyclopedia's neck stood up faster than Sitting Bull on a branding iron. He peered outside the tent.

It wasn't a bear. It was a man stumbling about in the moonlight. His hands were bound behind him. He was trying to speak, but the gag in his mouth turned his words into wild snorts.

Encyclopedia quickly untied him.

"I'm Jack Evans," the man panted. "Bring help! At campsite five. Robbers! Kidnappers!"

Robbers and kidnappers! The boys didn't waste time. Charlie, Fangs, and Pinky ran for the ranger station. Herb, Jody, and Billy made

Encyclopedia peered outside the tent.

for park headquarters.

Encyclopedia and Benny stayed with Mr. Evans, who talked excitedly during the five-minute walk to his campsite.

"I was camping with Roger Blake," said Mr. Evans. "I had just put a pot of coffee over the fire when a voice behind me said, 'Don't move. Don't turn around.' "

Mr. Evans ducked under a branch. Then he continued.

"From behind me I heard Roger say, 'Be careful. They both have guns.' I was ordered to lie face down. My hands and legs were tied, a gag fixed in my mouth, and my money and car keys were stolen."

Mr. Evans shook his fist in rage and went on.

" 'We're kidnapping your friend,' the voice behind me said. 'You'll hear from us tomorrow. We'll tell you where to leave the ransom money.' It took me about half an hour to kick my legs free. I ran for help—and found you boys."

"You didn't get a look at the kidnappers?" asked Benny.

"No," answered Mr. Evans. "I was facing the fire and the coffee pot. Everything happened behind me. Here we are . . ."

They had come to a large tent standing in a clearing. A few yards away, a coffee pot hung over a crackling fire.

Encyclopedia studied the ground. There were several footprints leading up to and away from the clearing. A few feet from the campfire was a piece of rope.

From the fire came a sudden, startling noise. The coffee had begun to boil over the sides of the pot and fell hissing on the burning logs beneath.

Encyclopedia stared at the fire thoughtfully.

"Do you see a clue or something?" asked Benny.

"Yes, a clue that Mr. Evans overlooked," answered Encyclopedia. "It solves the case of Roger Blake's kidnapping!"

WHAT WAS THE CLUE?

(Turn to page 90 for solution to The Case of the Bound Camper.)

The Case of the Junk Sculptor

Harold Finnegan wore eyeglasses, but none of the children called him "Four Eyes."

They called him "Four Wheels."

He was the only boy in the neighborhood who owned two bikes. He had a new bike for clear days and an old bike for rainy days.

However, he was riding his new bike when, on a rainy morning, he came to the Brown Detective Agency for help.

"Hi, Four Wheels," Encyclopedia said cheerfully.

"Call me Three Wheels," said Four Wheels. "I'm down to a bike and a half."

"Did you have a wreck?" asked Sally.

"No, somebody stole the front wheel of my old bike," he said. "I'm pretty sure the thief was Pablo Pizarro."

"How can you say such a thing?" demanded Sally. "Pablo is no thief. Pablo is a great artist! Pablo has feeling! Pablo has—"

"Pablo has my front wheel," insisted Four Wheels. "He stole it ten minutes ago."

Four Wheels rolled twenty-five cents on the gas can. "I'll need your help to get it back, Encyclopedia."

Encyclopedia took the case despite Sally's angry look. On the way to Pablo's house, Four Wheels told what had happened.

"Last night I started fixing my old bike," he said. "I took it all apart. When I went out to the garage this morning, I saw a boy running off with the wheel."

"You aren't sure it was Pablo?" said Sally.

"I never saw his face," admitted Four Wheels. He glanced at Encyclopedia. "You know what's been going on," he said.

Encyclopedia knew. For the past few weeks things had been disappearing from garages in the neighborhood. Strangely, the things were worthless—junk like broken mirrors, bits of wood, old newspapers, and rusty metal parts.

Encyclopedia had not told Sally, but Pablo had been seen hanging around the garages from which the junk disappeared.

The children reached Pablo's house, and Encyclopedia rang the bell. Pablo's mother leaned out a second floor window and called, "Come in. Pablo's in the attic."

Upstairs, Encyclopedia found the attic door locked. He pounded loudly. After a long moment Pablo opened the door.

"Enter," he said with a sweep of his arm. "Welcome to my studio."

Sally's hand fluttered to her mouth as she gazed upon Pablo. He wore a soft flat hat, a large bow for a necktie, and a dirty smock. "You're dressed just like a real artist!" she gasped in admiration.

"Of course," said Pablo with a careless shrug. "I am at work."

"He must be working at building a junk yard in his attic," thought Encyclopedia.

Junk—anything that stayed put—filled every corner. Some of it stood in newly painted mounds. Most just stood rusting away.

Four Wheels got to the point. "Where's my bicycle wheel?"

"Bicycle wheel?" repeated Pablo.

"The one you stole from my garage this morning!" growled Four Wheels.

"My dear fellow, you are talking rot," said Pablo. "It is true that I collect things to use in making my sculpture. But I do not steal!"

The boy artist walked across the attic.

"This is my newest piece," he said, pointing to a pile of wire clothes hangers, coffee pots, magazines, stove legs, an apple, and an automobile tire. "I shall paint it white and call it *Still Life with Apple*."

"Bravo!" squealed Sally in delight.

"This is my newest piece," Pablo said.

Encyclopedia and Four Wheels, being struck speechless, could only stare.

"I haven't been out of the house today," said Pablo. "So how could I steal a bicycle wheel? I've been sitting right here in this old chair working since breakfast. I got up only to answer your knock."

Encyclopedia studied the old chair. It was pulled close to *Still Life with Apple*. The chair was falling apart, but it looked better than Pablo's sculpture.

Small drops of white paint were splattered over the chair. The boy detective ran his hand lightly over the chair's cool seat and touched a few drops. They were dry.

"I don't see my wheel anyplace," whispered Four Wheels.

"Keep searching," said Encyclopedia. "You could hide a battleship in this mess."

Pablo had begun to show Sally around his studio. She followed him like a puppy and hung on every word.

"Upon finding an object in which something else is suggested, the artist uses his skill to bring the idea to fulfillment," said Pablo.

"Come again?" said Four Wheels from a corner.

The boy artist brought forth a board six feet long. On it were nailed a shovel, a fruit box, two smashed electric irons, a bent fan, and scraps of wallpaper.

"I call it *Man in Search of Himself*," said Pablo.

"It's beautiful!" exclaimed Sally. "It's exciting! It lifts me into a world of new ideas!"

Pablo's chest swelled. "I see you are not a beginner," he said. "You understand that what is important in art has nothing to do with cost, or prettiness, or even—"

"Cleanliness!" called out Four Wheels as he crawled behind a dusty heap of tires and chains.

"Don't pay any attention to him or Encyclopedia," said Sally. "They don't know great art when they see it!"

"Maybe not," said Encyclopedia. "But I know a thief when I see one, and Pablo is a thief!"

WHAT MADE ENCYCLOPEDIA SURE?

(Turn to page 91 for solution to The Case of the Junk Sculptor.)

The Case of the Treasure Map

Winslow Brant was Idaville's master snooper.

He snooped wherever a grown-up might have thrown away something valuable by mistake. No trash pile or ash can was safe from him.

Snooping had rewarded him well. Already he owned the finest collection of bottle caps and dead tennis balls in the neighborhood.

He wasn't snooping, however, when he came into the Brown Detective Agency. He was drooping.

"I nearly had it all," he moaned and sagged against the wall.

"Had what?" asked Encyclopedia.

"Treasure," said Winslow. "The dream of every great snooper—treasure beyond belief!"

"Your big chance slipped through your fingers?"

"No, it *ran*," said Winslow. He whipped out a piece of cloth. The colors had run together, making one large red smear. "It was a map showing where Henri La Farge buried some of his treasure!"

Everyone in the state knew of the famous pirate Henri La Farge. Two hundred years ago he had made his hideout among the small islands several miles south of Idaville. There, some-place, he supposedly buried a fortune.

"The map was in a broken music box I found yesterday morning on the Smith's trash pile," said Winslow. Then he told his sad story.

He had showed the map to Pete Alders, who was sixteen and owned a sailboat. Pete had agreed to take Winslow to the islands in return for a share of the treasure.

The boys had reached their destination after dark, and so they spent the night aboard ship. In the morning, Winslow had found the map drying on deck, ruined. Pete said he had used it to plug a leak during the night. In the dark, he had thought he was using a pillowcase.

"I'll bet Pete first made a copy of the map so he can have all the treasure for himself," said Winslow angrily. "After he brought me home, he probably returned to the islands."

"He won't find anything there but a sunburn," said Encyclopedia. He pointed to a tiny black smudge on the back of the map.

"Gosh, I never noticed that," said Winslow. "What is it?"

"It *was* writing," replied Encyclopedia. "It said 'New York World's Fair.' Your map was just a souvenir that cost fifty cents. My dad had one in the attic for years."

"Well, I'll be cow-kicked," said Winslow in disgust. "Worthless!" Suddenly his face lit up. "Pete's off digging for treasure—*he thinks*. Serves him right, the dirty double-crosser!"

"We don't know that Pete ruined your map on purpose," Encyclopedia said.

"I'll hire you," said Winslow. "If you find out that Pete copied my map, don't tell him the truth about it. Let him dig till he hears chopsticks."

Encyclopedia agreed, and two hours later the boys were heading toward the islands in a skiff borrowed from Sally Kimball's uncle.

They looked in at five islands before they spied Pete's sailboat. She was anchored in a small cove. One of her portholes was slightly open.

"Pete will be digging by a group of three coconut trees," said Winslow, hopping ashore. "The map showed a treasure chest was buried at the foot of the center tree."

After a short walk inland, the boys spied three coconut trees growing close together.

Pete was there, digging wearily in the hot sun.

"Boy, he looks ready to lean on his tongue," said Winslow happily.

"He's so greedy he believes those three trees are the ones on the map," replied Encyclopedia.

Pete was surprised to see the boys. He gave Winslow a weak smile as he climbed out of the hole. "You know I'll split what I find with you," he said nervously.

"Sure, Pete," said Winslow. "And I see you fixed the sailboat. I never did ask you where the leak was."

"Well . . . ah . . . it was . . . ah . . . a porthole," said Pete. "It wouldn't close."

"One porthole was stuck," said Winslow. "I remember." His words seemed to put Pete more at ease.

The older boy said, "After you lay down in the cabin last night, I stayed on deck checking things. I saw that we had anchored at low tide. In a little while, the tide started coming in."

Pete was digging wearily in the hot sun.

"You see very well in the dark," said Encyclopedia.

"There was moonlight," said Pete. "I could see the high water mark on the shore. It was then about two and a half feet above the water level."

"What has high and low tide got to do with my map getting wet and ruined?" demanded Winslow.

"The tide rose about five inches an hour," said Pete. "The portholes are eighteen inches above the waterline. In less than four hours the tide would rise to the open porthole. Water would pour in and sink the boat."

"So you plugged the porthole and saved the boat," said Winslow. "With my map!"

"That was a mistake, I told you," said Pete. "The cabin was so dark I thought I had a pillowcase. Honest."

Winslow looked uncertain. He turned to Encyclopedia and whispered, "Pete may be telling the truth."

"No, he wet your map on purpose to keep you from finding what he thought was buried treasure," said Encyclopedia. "His story about the porthole doesn't hold water!"

WHY NOT?

(Turn to page 92 for solution to The Case of the Treasure Map.)

The Case of the Five Clues

Shortly after four o'clock on Wednesday afternoon Jane Foster came into the Brown Detective Agency. Her eyes were brimming with tears.

She looked from Sally to Encyclopedia. "You've got to help me," she said. "Somebody robbed my dad's store while I was minding it!"

Mr. Foster owned the Sunset Five-and-Dime. Encyclopedia bought his school supplies and bubble gum there.

"You should report a robbery to the police," he said.

"I can't!" said Jane, blowing her nose. "I

don't want my dad to find out I was careless. I left the side door unlocked!"

She put a quarter on the gas can beside Encyclopedia. "Please help me get the money back!"

"I'll do what I can, but I don't have much time," said Encyclopedia. "My mom will want me in for dinner in two hours."

"We don't even have two hours," said Jane. "My dad will be back from Glenn City in an hour!"

Gloom filled the Brown Agency. One hour! Could Encyclopedia learn enough in one hour to solve the robbery?

"We'd better get started," he said. He spoke with a cheerfulness he didn't feel. "Don't worry, Jane. Everything will turn out fine."

To save time, the three children did not use their bikes to get to town. They rode the Number 3 bus. On the way, Jane told Encyclopedia all she knew about the robbery.

"Wednesdays my dad closes the store at

three o'clock," she said. "Today he was in a hurry to get to Glenn City. So he left the store five minutes early. He told me to close up.

"I locked the front and back doors," Jane continued. "Then I went to the washroom to comb my hair. Suddenly I heard the cash register ring. I hurried out and saw someone race out the side door."

"How many doors does the store have?" asked Sally.

"Three—front, back, and side," answered Jane. "The side door is seldom used. I just forgot to lock it."

"Did you get a look at the thief's face?" asked Encyclopedia.

"No," said Jane. "Everything happened so fast. I don't know if the thief was a man or a woman, or a boy or girl."

The bus had come to their stop. The three children got off and walked to a two-story white building. The Sunset Five-and-Dime took up the entire first floor except for a brown wood door at one end.

"What door is that?" asked Encyclopedia.

"It leads to living quarters above the store," said Jane.

She unlocked the front door of the store. Sally and Encyclopedia followed her inside.

Encyclopedia stared at the counter before the cash register. On the counter were a pack of rubber bands, a can of oil, a magnet, a sheet of sandpaper, and a pack of blotters.

"Were those things on the counter when you locked the front and back doors at closing time?" he asked.

"I don't remember them," said Jane. "Are they clues?"

Encyclopedia didn't answer. Instead he asked to see the side door through which the thief had fled.

The side door opened into a hall. At one end was the staircase going up to the living quarters

"Are they clues?" said Jane.

above the store. At the other end was the brown door which opened onto the street.

"Is that brown door kept locked?" asked Encyclopedia.

"It locks by itself when it shuts," said Jane.

"Then the thief must be someone who lives upstairs," said Encyclopedia. "He had to have a key to get past the brown door."

"Do you know who did it?" exclaimed Sally.

"Not yet," said Encyclopedia.

He paused thoughtfully. Then he said, "The thief came down the stairs shortly before closing. He—let's say the thief was a man—didn't know Jane had closed the store a few minutes early today."

"You mean the thief didn't plan on robbery?" asked Sally.

"Correct," said Encyclopedia. "The thief took five things he wanted and went to the cash register to pay for them."

Sally cried, "When he realized he was alone

in the store, he decided to rob it. He didn't know Jane was in the washroom!"

"That's how it looks," said Encyclopedia. "When the cash register rang as he opened it, he got scared. He fled with the money. But he left behind the five things he had wanted to buy."

"Who lives above the store?" Sally asked Jane.

"The front two apartments belong to Mr. Corey and Mr. Evans," said Jane. "Each lives alone. Mr. Corey works for the Health Department. Mr. Evans is the night watchman at the First Federal Bank."

"Who lives in the rear apartments?" asked Encyclopedia.

"Mrs. O'Quinn lives with her daughter Mary in one apartment," said Jane. "Mrs. O'Quinn works as a cleaning woman and takes in sewing at night. The other apartment has been empty since the Andersons moved away two months ago."

"Can't you tell us anything more about the people upstairs?" asked Sally anxiously.

"I'm sorry," said Jane. "I don't know any more. I don't see them often."

"It doesn't matter," said Encyclopedia. "You've told us enough."

WHO WAS THE THIEF?

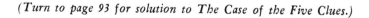

(Turn to page 93 for solution to The Case of the Five Clues.)

The Case of the Gold Rush

As Encyclopedia biked past the empty lot on Rock Garden Lane, he saw Nathan Winslow swinging a pickax at top speed.

The boy detective braked to a halt. "Hey, Nathan," he called. "What are you doing?"

"What does it look like?" said Nathan. "I'm digging. Now leave me alone. Go wash an elephant or something. I have to practice."

His snappish answer surprised Encyclopedia. A quiet boy of nine, Nathan was known for his good manners. In fact, he was so polite he never visited Echo Valley. He didn't want to talk back.

Encyclopedia wheeled his bike onto the sidewalk. He tried again. "What are you practicing?"

"Digging rocks if you must know," said Nathan. "I've got to show Wilford Wiggins I can help him dig for gold."

Wilford Wiggins was a high school dropout. He had more get-rich-quick ideas every minute than fingerprints on a volleyball. Encyclopedia kept busy stopping Wilford from cheating the children of the neighborhood.

"Wilford says he found a gold mine," guessed Encyclopedia.

"Yep," said Nathan. "The mine is out west someplace. Any kid with five dollars can buy a share of it. Since I'm broke, I thought I could work for a share."

Nathan put down his pickax. "Wilford's holding a meeting at ten o'clock in South Park," he said. "I'd better get over there."

"Wilford didn't tell me about the meeting," said Encyclopedia.

"He hates you like poison," said Nathan.

"What's like poison is Wilford's big talk," said Encyclopedia. "But it can't hurt you if you don't swallow it."

Nathan suddenly looked worried.

"Maybe Wilford's gold mine is as phoney as bull's wool," he said uneasily. "You'd better come to the meeting, Encyclopedia. You might save the day."

Encyclopedia agreed to go. On the way, Nathan apologized.

"I'm sorry I was so fresh to you," he said. "I guess I wasn't myself."

"Forget it," said Encyclopedia. "The shine of gold can be worse than a close shave. It has made lots of people lose their heads."

At South Park, Encyclopedia saw a crowd of children gathered around the statue of Abraham Lincoln.

Wilford Wiggins was leaning against the

Wilford was about to start his sales talk.

statue, trying to look honest. He was about to start his sales talk.

The children stepped closer. They were eager to hear how he would make them dirty rich.

"You've all heard about the gold strike out west," said Wilford. "My partner, Digger Dan, found the mine. But we need money to buy a mule. So I'm going to make each of you a junior partner for a mere five dollars."

"Sure, sure," said Bugs Meany, pushing his way to the front. "I'll be so rich my little sister will have to quit piano lessons and take up playing the cash register!"

"That's a fact, kid," replied Wilford.

"Exactly where is your gold mine?" asked Benny Breslin.

"I wish I could tell you," answered Wilford. "But I'm too good an American. If I told, all the people in the east would rush out west. The whole country would tip into the Pacific Ocean and sink."

"Aw, cut the comedy or get off the air," sneered Bugs.

"If you found a gold mine," said Hector Conklin, "why didn't you dig enough gold to buy a mule? Why do you need our money?"

"I'll tell you, friend," said Wilford. "Six months ago my partner, Digger Dan, went into the hills looking for gold. He took along his faithful mule Queenie to carry supplies.

"Digger Dan has been looking for gold for thirty-three years," went on Wilford. "This trip his bad luck ended. He hit the mother lode, the richest gold strike ever! But did he get greedy and haul it away? No! Queenie was about to have a baby and Queenie came before worldly riches."

Wilford paused to let his words settle upon the animal lovers in the crowd.

Then he went on. "Digger Dan waited at the gold mine. He needed Queenie to carry back the gold. At last, Queenie had her baby, Strike-It-Rich. But instead of growing stronger, Queenie grew weaker. Days passed. Food and water ran low. Little Strike-It-Rich died. Five days later Queenie died, too."

Wilford bowed his head. When he looked up again, there was a tear in his eye.

He said, "Digger Dan might have taken a fortune in gold from the mine if he were heartless. He might have made two or three quick trips back to town even though Queenie wasn't fit for heavy work."

The children were silent. Jane Foster was crying. So was Lucy Fibbs.

"Now you know why we need money," said Wilford. "Digger Dan didn't bring back enough gold to buy a shoelace. But if I can raise the money, he'll be able to buy another mule, go back to the hills, and start working the mine."

The children pressed around Wilford, waving their money. Bugs Meany bought the first share. He biked off as pleased with himself as a millionaire.

Before anyone else could buy a share, Encyclopedia held up his hands.

"Don't throw away your money," he said. "There is no gold mine!"

HOW DID ENCYCLOPEDIA KNOW?

(Turn to page 94 for solution to The Case of the Gold Rush.)

The Case of the Flying Boy

Encyclopedia was biking past Casper Keane's house when he saw something on the roof. It was Casper.

"Hey, come down!" shouted Encyclopedia.

"Don't bother me," said Casper. He had a paper wing tied to each arm. He closed his eyes and began to rock.

"What are you doing?" said Encyclopedia.

"I'm hypnotizing myself," answered Casper.

"Can't you hypnotize yourself on the ground?"

"Once I get myself hypnotized, I'm going to tell myself I'm a bird," said Casper, who was eight and a great believer. "Then I'll fly."

"You'll fly like a stone kite," said Encyclopedia.

"Nope, it's going to work," said Casper. "Buck Barkdull has flown—"

"Nobody can fly!" screamed Encyclopedia. "Jump off the roof and you'll find out what an anchor does."

"Aw, you shouldn't have said that," said Casper. He climbed down. "Still, I'm glad you stopped me. I was losing faith."

"What made you think you could fly?" asked Encyclopedia.

"Buck Barkdull said so," answered Casper. "He sold me these wings for six dollars. He wanted another six dollars to hypnotize me. I didn't have any more money. So I borrowed a book on hypnotism at the library."

"If Buck could fly, he wouldn't sell you the secret for a few dollars," pointed out Encyclopedia. "He would sell it to the Army for millions!"

"But Pete Connell said he *saw* Buck fly!" said Casper.

"Pete and Buck are probably in this together," said Encyclopedia. "Remember what happened at the high school last year?"

Casper nodded. Buck had stolen the answers to a history test. Pete had sold them to students for two dollars. Both boys had been kicked out of school for a term.

"I've been a sap," mumbled Casper. "I guess I wanted to fly more than think. Could you get my six dollars back?"

"I can try," said Encyclopedia. "Let's go talk with Pete Connell. He isn't as smart as Buck."

"Let's talk with Buck," said Casper. "Pete was on the wrestling team. He might tie us in a knot."

Encyclopedia decided Casper was right. It

was better to be outsmarted than to have your feet hooked over your ears. The two boys went to see Buck.

He was sitting on his front porch carving fifty-cent pieces out of wood. He listened calmly as Encyclopedia asked him to return Casper's six dollars.

"Why should I?" he demanded. "If you don't *believe* you can fly, you won't fly. You've got to have faith, baby."

Encyclopedia pressed him till Buck agreed to prove he could fly. He told the two boys to meet him in the small woods behind Mr. Walker's nursery after dark.

The boys reached the woods as night fell. "It's so dark in here I couldn't see Buck if he flew past my nose in a garbage truck," said Casper.

Suddenly strange noises came from up in a nearby tree. Buck Barkdull slid to the ground.

"Did you see that!" he cried. "A crash land-ing! Am I lucky I wasn't killed!' "

"We didn't see a thing," said Casper.

"It was so dark I flew smack into that tree," said Buck, removing his wings. "Otherwise, I'd have landed like a butterfly at your feet."

"You were up in the tree all the time," said Encyclopedia.

"Is that so?" sneered Buck. "It just so happens that I have a witness. Pete Connell saw me take off from my attic window."

"Why don't you take off right now?" said Encyclopedia.

"Because I have to start from up high," answered Buck. "I could fly from one of these trees, but the branches would get in my way. Besides, my wings are broken, and I don't have an extra pair."

The arguing continued. Buck would not give back Casper's six dollars, and Encyclopedia would not leave without the money. Buck finally threw up his hands.

"I'll show you where I begin my flights," Buck said.

"I'll show you where I begin my flights and nothing more," he said. "After that, if you bother me again, I'll punch you in the belly when your back is turned."

"Ouch," Casper whispered over and over as they followed Buck home.

Pete Connell was waiting outside Buck's house. Buck winked at his pal slyly.

Immediately Pete exclaimed, "What a flight! You soared like an eagle. Buck Barkdull, you're greater than Lindbergh!"

Buck unlocked the front door. "My parents are away for the day, and I'm here alone," he said.

He led the way up to the attic. He turned on the light and walked to the one window.

"This is my launching pad," he said, rolling up the shade and opening the window. "I stand here and get myself in the mood—that's the important part. I hypnotize myself. When I feel ready, I jump out head first."

"Suppose you've made a mistake?" asked

Encyclopedia. "What if you're not fully hypnotized when you jump?"

"I fall and land in those bushes," said Buck, pointing to bushes growing by the house.

"Did you fall tonight?" asked Casper.

"Naw, it was a perfect flight," said Buck. "Once I was through the window, I flew straight for the woods without falling a foot."

"It was beautiful!" sang Pete Connell.

"I don't believe a word," whispered Casper. "But how can we *prove* the wings and the hypnotism are fakes?"

"We don't have to," replied Encyclopedia. "Buck already has proved that for us!"

WHAT WAS BUCK'S MISTAKE?

(Turn to page 95 for solution to The Case of the Flying Boy.)

The Case of the Foot Warmer

Melvin Pugh was always inventing something. When he came into the Brown Detective Agency, he looked as if he had invented a new way to walk.

His knees didn't bend, and he moved spread-legged, as if his feet were stuck to railroad tracks.

"Golly, Melvin, have you been horseback riding?" asked Sally.

"No, I hate horses," said Melvin. He snorted into a horn that stuck out of his shirt. "And I hate cold weather. Nobody does anything about horses. But I have done something about cold weather."

Encyclopedia got up enough nerve to ask, "What?"

"I'll show you," said Melvin. "First, I have to take off my clothes."

He undid his belt.

"Melvin!" shrieked Sally.

"I've got a bathing suit on," Melvin assured her. He stepped out of his trousers and pulled off his shirt.

"Behold!" he said. "The Melvin Pugh hot-air foot warmer!"

Encyclopedia and Sally beheld.

A rubber tube ran down each leg to Melvin's shoes. At the top, the tubes joined and fed into the horn. The horn was kept in place by a strap around Melvin's neck.

"You blow into the horn," explained Melvin. "The heat of your breath passes down to your feet where it is needed."

"It sure is simple," said Encyclopedia. He felt the tubes. They were hard and stiff as iron.

"I have to find softer tubes," said Melvin.

"Wearing these, I feel like a wishbone. And I can't bend an inch."

"When you can warm your feet and touch your toes at the same time, you'll make a million dollars," said Sally.

"My warmer is particularly useful in winter on cold floors, frozen ground, and icy sidewalks," said Melvin proudly.

"You ought to test it in the winter," suggested Encyclopedia. "You could give yourself a terrible hotfoot in this summer heat."

"I just tested it in Archer's Toy Shop," said Melvin. "It worked like a charm."

The toy shop was the coldest place in Idaville during the summer. Mr. Archer, who owned the shop, kept the air conditioner going full blast.

"A great choice, the toy shop," said Encyclopedia. "You looked over the latest-model car kits while you tried out the tubes, eh?"

"You guessed it," said Melvin. "A person can loose his mind doing nothing but breath-

"You little thief!" bellowed Mr. Archer.

ing on his feet. Will I be glad to get out of this rig. Give me a hand, will you?"

Encyclopedia helped him take off the foot warmer. As Melvin was pulling up his trousers, a car drove past. It slowed, backed up, and stopped in front of the Brown Detective Agency.

Mr. Archer got out. He shook his finger at Melvin angrily.

"You little thief!" bellowed Mr. Archer. "I knew you couldn't get far!"

"Thief?" said Melvin. "Me?"

"I've thought all along you're the one who has been shoplifting in my store," said Mr. Archer. "Today you stole two air rifles worth eleven dollars and eighty cents apiece!"

Melvin looked at Encyclopedia pleadingly. "I didn't steal anything except cold air," he said.

"I don't want to report you to the police," said Mr. Archer. "Just give me back the rifles and stay away from my store."

"Gee whiz, Mr. Archer," said Encyclopedia, "why do you think Melvin stole them?"

"Five minutes after he left my store, I went to get a rifle for Mrs. Bowen. Two were missing," said Mr. Archer.

"I noticed a redheaded kid looking at the rifles," said Melvin meekly.

"Billy Griffith?" said Mr. Archer. "Billy is a nice boy. He *buys* things."

"But you didn't actually see Melvin steal the rifles," said Sally.

"No, but that was because of Mrs. Hall's baby," said Mr. Archer. "The baby can't walk, but he crawls like a flash."

"I don't understand at all," said Sally.

"Mrs. Hall put down the baby to pay me for a doll," said Mr. Archer. "The baby crawled away. We found him in the back of the store. Melvin was holding him."

"You don't think Melvin was trying to steal the baby!" howled Sally.

"Certainly not," snapped Mr. Archer. "I

was so glad to find the baby unharmed that I didn't watch Melvin for several minutes."

"That's when you think he stole the rifles?" asked Encyclopedia.

"He stole them," said Mr. Archer. "When I saw Melvin next, he was going out the door. He walked as if his legs were dipped in concrete. He must have had a rifle hidden in each trouser leg!"

Sally picked up the hot-air foot warmer. "He had this in his trousers!" she said. "It's an invention. It warms the feet."

Mr. Archer stared at the foot warmer in disbelief. He scratched his head.

"If Melvin isn't the thief, who is?" he said. "I'm missing two rifles, and I want them back!"

"I'll have them back in an hour," promised Encyclopedia.

WHY WAS ENCYCLOPEDIA SO SURE?

(Turn to page 96 for solution to The Case of the Foot Warmer.)

Solution to *The Case of the Electric Clock*

Gil had only the electric clock in his bedroom. "I don't have another clock," he told Encyclopedia.

But Bugs claimed that he had heard the clock still ticking when he passed Gil's bedroom on the way home.

That was Bug's lie!

Bugs had thought to prove the thief was someone else, someone who came later and unplugged the clock.

However, Bugs could not have heard the clock still ticking.

Why?

Because he forgot a simple fact: *Electric clocks don't tick!*

Trapped by his own lie, Bugs gave Gil back the telescope.

And he returned all the dimes he had been paid for the moon man show.

Solution to *The Case of the Bird Watcher*

Bugs had tried to get Encyclopedia in trouble, but two facts ruined his story.

First, the Dade River ran due east to the ocean. Second, Bugs said he walked toward the ocean at sunrise, watching the birds along the river.

A real bird watcher, however, never walks east early in the morning!

Walking into the rising sun, the bird watcher would see the birds merely as dark shapes against the bright sky. At sunrise the real bird watcher walks west so that the sun's full light comes from behind him and falls on the birds.

Tripped up by his own story, Bugs confessed.

He had sent Encyclopedia the letter signed "Bill." After the detective had tired of waiting for "Bill" and had left Mr. Dunning's station, Bugs had let the air out of the tires himself.

Solution to *The Case of the Kidnapped Pigs*

The kidnapper was Carl, who owned Alfred.

Alfred had finished second to Lucy's pig Gwendoline at last year's pet show. Carl wanted Alfred to win this year.

So he "kidnapped" both pigs. Just before the pet show, he was going to say that Alfred escaped and found his way home.

Carl tried to put the blame on the Hurricanes. He stole Harry's cap. Then he made up the story about the kidnapper needing another dime for the telephone. That would show the caller was a child, not a grown-up, he thought.

But Carl could not have dialed the kidnapper back. There is no such number as ZA 6-7575 because there is no Z on the telephone dial!

Caught in his own lie, Carl returned Gwendoline to Lucy.

And the next day Gwendoline again won the obedience contest at the pet show.

Solution to *The Case of the Bound Camper*

The clue was the coffee pot.

From the time Mr. Evans claimed he had put the pot of coffee over the fire until he returned with Encyclopedia, more than forty minutes passed.

After forty minutes on the fire, so much water in the pot would have boiled away that none could have boiled over the top. Yet boil over it did—before Encyclopedia's eyes!

That meant the coffee pot was put on the fire long after Mr. Evans said it was.

Having given himself away, Mr. Evans confessed. He was really part of the kidnap gang.

He had wanted a simple story. So he said he didn't see the kidnappers because he was busy with the coffee pot.

Actually, he had put the coffee over the fire just before his partners gagged him and tied his hands to make him look like an innocent victim, and sent him off to find "help."

Solution to *The Case of the Junk Sculptor*

As soon as Encyclopedia touched the old chair, he knew that Pablo had stolen Four Wheels' bike wheel.

The boy detective found the drops of white paint were dry and—what else?

He found the seat was *cool.*

If Pablo had been sitting in the chair all morning, as he claimed, the seat would have been *warm* from his body heat!

Shown his mistake, Pablo confessed to stealing the bike wheel and to taking junk from other garages.

He returned the bike wheel. He tried to return the junk, but no one wanted it returned.

Indeed, once the people of the neighborhood learned that Pablo needed junk to make his sculpture, they let him hunt in their garages whenever he liked.

"I never thought to ask," said Pablo.

Solution to *The Case of the Treasure Map*

Encyclopedia knew that Pete had ruined Winslow's map after first making a copy to use himself.

The boy detective saw through Pete's story about the porthole immediately.

Pete claimed that the tide was rising "about five inches an hour." That part was true.

But Pete also said that he was afraid the water would rise above the open porthole, which was "eighteen inches above the water line" when he had dropped anchor at low tide.

However, the rising tide would never have reached the open porthole even if it rose twice as fast.

For the boat, floating on the tide, would have risen too!

Winslow let Pete dig up the island for another hour before telling him the "treasure" map was nothing but a souvenir of the World's Fair.

Solution to *The Case of the Five Clues*

Encyclopedia saw that the strange collection of things on the counter pointed to Mrs. O'Quinn. She took in sewing, remember?

She used the *can of oil* to oil her sewing machine.

She stitched through the *blotter* several times after each oiling. This removed the danger of getting oil spots on her material.

She stitched through the *sandpaper* a few times to sharpen her needles.

She used the *magnet* to pick up dropped pins.

She kept a *rubber band* around her spools of thread to keep them from getting tangled.

The real thief was Mrs. O'Quinn's daughter Mary, fourteen. Mary had been sent downstairs to the store. When she got back, she told her mother the store was closed.

Mrs. O'Quinn made Mary return the money at once.

Solution to *The Case of the Gold Rush*

Wilford Wiggins had a problem.

He had to show why he needed money even though his partner, Digger Dan, had supposedly discovered a gold mine.

So Wilford made up a story.

The story was aimed at showing that no gold had been carried from the mine. The gold had to be moved on the back of an animal, and Digger Dan had lost his mule, Queenie.

But Wilford made a mistake.

He told a story in which Queenie the mule had a baby, Strike-It-Rich.

Immediately, Encyclopedia knew the story was untrue.

Wilford didn't know that neither Queenie nor any other mule can have a baby mule.

A mule is the offspring of a female horse and a male ass. Mules simply cannot have young of their own!

Solution to *The Case of the Flying Boy*

Buck said he had taken off by jumping through the attic window.

"Once I was through the window, I flew straight for the woods," he said.

That meant he had not come back to the window.

But when he showed the window to Encyclopedia, it was closed, and the shade was drawn!

He could not have jumped through a shade and a closed window!

Nobody could have come up to the attic and closed the window after he flew away. He was living alone for the day, and the house was locked.

Buck didn't like being found out by Encyclopedia. But he returned the six dollars to Casper.

And he retired from the business of selling flying lessons.

Solution to *The Case of the Foot Warmer*

Encyclopedia knew Melvin was the thief.

The fact that he was holding Mrs. Hall's baby in his arms at the back of the store gave him away.

In order to pick up the baby, Melvin had to be able to bend over.

So he was not wearing the foot warmer in the store. Remember, the tubes of the foot warmer were "hard and stiff as iron."

Melvin confessed.

He had got the rifles out of the store by sticking one in each trouser leg, as Mr. Archer suspected.

After hiding the rifles, he had put on his hot air foot warmer. Then he had gone to the Brown Detective Agency. He had hoped to make Encyclopedia believe that he had walked out of the store stiffly because he wore the foot warmer.

Encyclopedia returned the two rifles.